NIKI DALY has been writing and illustrating award-winning picture books for nearly 30 years, both in South Africa and abroad. His 1986 book, *Not So Fast Songololo*, winner of the Katrine Harries Award and a U.S. Parent's Choice Award, paved the way for post-apartheid South African children's books. *Why the Sun and Moon Live in the Sky*, winner of the Anne Izard Story Teller's Choice Award, was chosen by the New York Times Literary Supplement as One of the Year's Best Illustrated Books in 1996. Among his many Frances Lincoln books, *Once Upon a Time* was an Honor Winner in the U.S. Children's Africana Book Awards of 2004. *Jamela's Dress* – first in the Jamela series – was another milestone book, chosen by the ALA as a Notable Children's Book, by Booklist as one of the Top 10 African American Picture Books of 2000, and winner of both the Children's Literature Choice Award and the Parent's Choice Silver Award.

Jamela

Jamela

Jamela

Jamela

Jamela

For the brave children of the Red Cross Hospital School, Cape Town

Where's Jamela? copyright © Frances Lincoln Limited 2004
Text and illustrations copyright © Niki Daly 2004
By arrangement with The Inkman, Cape Town, South Africa
Hand-lettering by Andrew van der Merwe

First published in Great Britain in 2004 by
Frances Lincoln Children's Books, 4 Torriano Mews,
Torriano Avenue, London NW5 2RZ
www.franceslincoln.com

With thanks to Kathy Kavanagh and Leela Pienaar of the
Dictionary Unit for South African English, Rhodes University

First paperback edition 2005

British Library Cataloguing in Publication Data available on request

ISBN 978-1-84507-106-6

Set in Bembo

Printed in Singapore

9 8 7 6 5 4 3 2

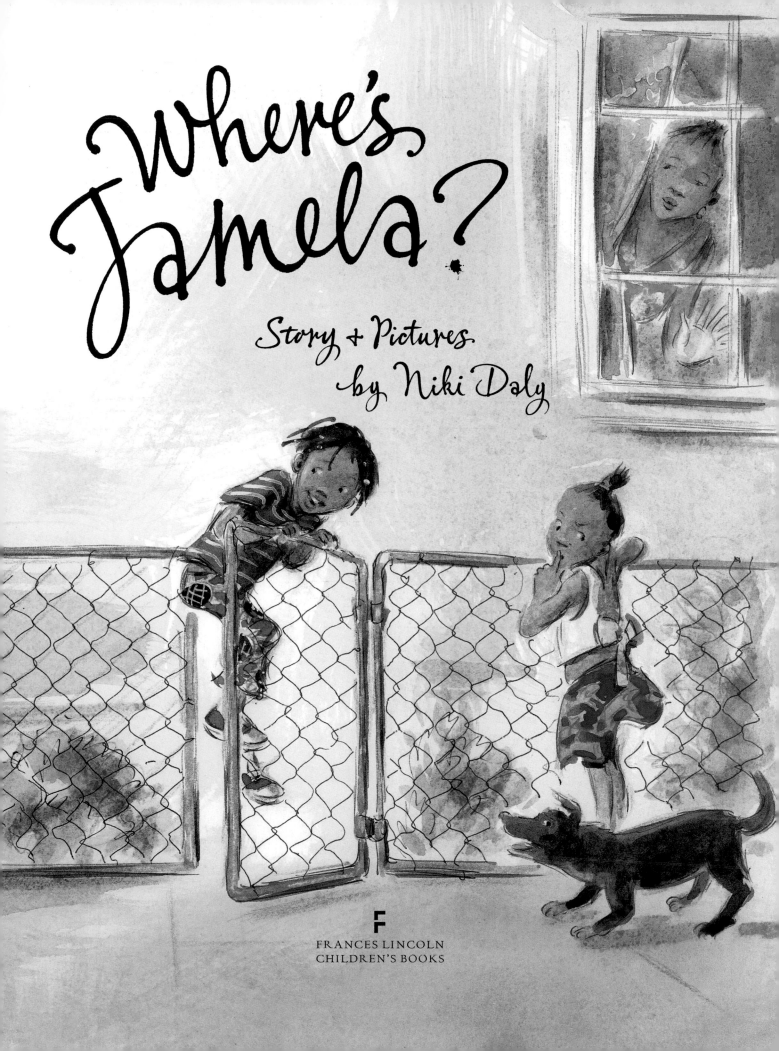

Where's Jamela?

Story & Pictures
by Niki Daly

F

FRANCES LINCOLN
CHILDREN'S BOOKS

"I've got it! I've got it!" sang Jamela's mama as she danced around the kitchen table, clutching a letter.

"What have you got, Mama?" asked Jamela.

"A new job and a new place to stay," said Mama. "Oh, Jamela, we are going to be very happy in our new house."

"But I like this one, Mama," Jamela said, frowning.

"You will *love* the new house," said Mama. "There's a nice room for you and one for Gogo, if she'd like to stay with us."

Jamela wasn't happy about Mama's plans. She loved their old house with its squeaky front gate to swing on. She loved her bedroom window and the world she saw out of it. She loved the street sounds – Greasy Hands revving up old cars, Mrs Zibi shouting at her chickens, dogs barking and children playing. At suppertime there was always a nice smell of cooking.

And high above, in the evening sky, a star looked down
on Jamela as she lay in bed.

A few days later, Gogo came around to help. She said
it would be lovely to move in with Mama and Jamela,
as long as she could take her piano.

"No problem," said Mama. "Greasy Hands is going to use
a big truck to move everything."

Mama and Gogo chatted about Mama's new job and the
new house and how happy they were all going to be. Jamela
didn't like all the talk about new things.

When Gogo saw how unhappy Jamela looked, she smiled
and said, "Come, Jamela, you can help me pack."

Jamela started wrapping the teapot, but it got all twisted up in newspaper. Suddenly it fell right out of her hands and crashed on to the floor.

"Oh! Jamela!" cried Mama. "That's my only teapot!"

Jamela felt terrible.

Gogo patted her and said quietly, "Why don't you go and pack your things, sweetie?"

Jamela put Christmas, her chicken, into the special cage
that Mrs Zibi had given her for the move.

Then she carefully wrapped
her pink butterfly tea-set
in toilet paper so that
nothing would break.

She packed it safely
into her little
red suitcase.

Mama brought a big cardboard box and wrote on it

Jamela's Box

Jamela packed her red suitcase into the box, then her books, then her dolls and finally all her school things.

By now, Jamela was fed up with packing. There was too much thumping, bumping and fussing going on around her.

So she climbed into the box, pulled down the flaps
and packed herself away.

Soon she
was fast asleep.

Meanwhile, Greasy Hands and his friend Lucky
turned up and started carrying all the boxes, bags
and suitcases out to the truck.

"Be careful with my precious things," said Mama.
"Don't scratch my piano!" cried Gogo.
"Don't worry – be happy!" joked Greasy Hands.

After a lot of hard work, the truck was almost loaded.

"Don't forget this one, Greasy Hands," said Gogo.
Greasy Hands lifted the box and carried it
carefully to the truck.

"Be careful!" said Mama, as Greasy Hands passed the big box to Lucky.

"*Yebo!*" said Lucky. "I know —
it's precious!"

Then they were ready to go. Gogo sat in the front with Greasy Hands while Mama and Lucky sat on boxes at the back of the truck.

"Hold on tight!" called Greasy Hands, as he started the truck.

But before they could move off, Mama shouted,
"Wait, wait! Where's Jamela?"

Everyone rushed back into the house. Mama called loudly,
"Jamela! Jamela!" They looked in every room.

"Maybe she's run away,"
said Gogo. "She was very unhappy
about us moving to a new house."
"Oh, Gogo, do you think so?"
said Mama. She looked very worried.

Mama and Gogo ran down the road. When they reached
Miss Style's salon, they asked the ladies, "Have you seen Jamela?"
"No," said the ladies. "What's up?"

Next, they asked Mrs Zibi, "Have you seen Jamela?"
"No!" said Mrs Zibi. "Is Jamela up to her tricks again?"

Meanwhile, Greasy Hands called the police. When Mama and Gogo returned to the truck, a sergeant was busy taking a description of Jamela.

"She's about six years old. She's wearing funky trousers and sporty red shoes. She's got beaded braids. She's a really cool kid," explained Greasy Hands.

The sergeant looked up from his notebook, then grinned. "Like the one sitting in the box?" he said, pointing with his pen.

They all turned round…

…and there was Jamela – awake at last!

The neighbours cheered. Gogo was so happy that she climbed on to the truck, opened her piano and started to play.

Everyone began to sing and dance. It was a going-away song.
Jamela could see tears in Mama's eyes. It was time to go.

Later that afternoon, the truck pulled up outside a little house
in the suburbs. Mama was right. It was a very nice house –
with a wooden door, two windows,
a curvy fence and a front gate.

"Listen, Mama… it squeaks!"
squealed Jamela.

When everything was unloaded, everyone looked tired and hot.

"*Shu!*" said Gogo, "I'd love a cup of tea, but we don't have a teapot."

Jamela remembered the broken teapot. Suddenly she had an idea! She found her suitcase and took out her pink plastic tea-set with butterflies. Excitedly, she filled the teapot at the new kitchen sink.

Then she called, "Mama! Gogo! Everyone! Come and have some tea!"

Jamela poured and handed everyone a tiny cup.
"Thank you, Jamela," said Gogo. "This is just
what we needed."

That night, Jamela lay in bed looking out of the window. Somewhere, a meowing cat was driving some poor dog mad. There was a spicy smell coming from The Bombay Take-Away. Across the road, *kwaito* music started to play. When Gogo and Mama came in to say goodnight, Gogo said, "*Shu*, this place is crazy with life."

"Well, it's home now, Ma," said Mama. "What do you think, Jamela?"

High above the rooftops, Jamela saw her little star in its right place up in the evening sky. She smiled and said, "I think it's going to be all right, Mama."

Mama kissed her goodnight. Gogo gave her a tickle. Then Jamela rolled over and went to sleep in her new room in her new home – under the same old sky.

Glossary

kwaito (Xhosa/Afrikaans) "quite-oh": type of South African pop music

shu! (probably Xhosa, Zulu or S. Sotho): an expression of surprise, wonder or relief

yebo (Zulu), "yeah-baw": Yes, I agree